BEE TREE

DRAGON'S LAI...

OWL'S HOUSE

CHRISTOPHER ROBIN'S HOUSE

EEYORE'S GLOOMY PLACE

N
W E
S

Around the Year With Pooh

Walt Disney Productions'

Around the Year With Pooh

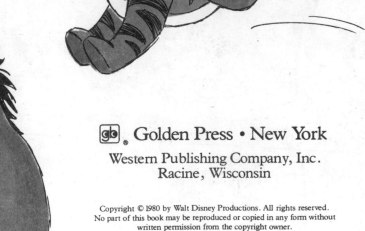

gb® Golden Press • New York

Western Publishing Company, Inc.
Racine, Wisconsin

CONTENTS

The March Wind 7

Star Gazers 9

March Birthday: Pooh 10

Poem by Winnie O'Pooh 11

Kite Flying 12

April Birthday: Sir Brian 13

An April Poem 15

Easter Eggs 16

Pooh's Favorite Flower 17

May 1: May Day 18

May Birthday: Dragon 20

June Birthday:
    Christopher Robin 24

The Longest Day 25

Star Gazers 27

July Birthday: Kanga 28

Hundred Acre Wood Records 29

Camping Out 30

August 15: Hay Fever
    Season Begins 32

August Birthday:
    Very Small Beetle 33

More Hundred Acre Wood
    Records 34

FALL

September Birthday: Roo 37

The First Day of School 38

The Harvest Season 40

October Birthday: Rabbit 42

October 31: Halloween 43

A Weather Report 45

Star Gazers 46

November Birthday: Piglet . . 47

WINTER

December Birthday: Owl 50

December 24: Christmas Eve . 52

January 1: New Year's Day . . . 54

January Birthday: Tigger 56

Star Gazers 57

February 14: St. Valentine's
      Day 58

February Birthday: Eeyore . . . 59

SPRING

"Spring is a bouncy time of year," said Tigger.

Owl nodded wisely. "Did you know that spring comes from a very old word for 'rising?'" he asked.

"Look!" said Pooh. "There's a crocus rising!" And he bent to sniff the first flower of spring.

March

The March Wind

The March wind was rising. And so was Piglet, clinging to the tail of his flyaway kite. "Help! Help!" he cried, sailing into the top of a tall, skinny pine tree.

"Hang on, Piglet!" shouted Tigger.

"We'll get you down," said Christopher Robin.

But how to reach him? There were no branches near where Piglet was stuck.

"Do I hear a damsel in distress?" shouted Sir Brian, clanking up in his armor.

"It's a *piglet* in distress," explained Pooh.

"Then, forsooth, it's Sir Brian to the rescue!" cried the knight.

"If you'll lend me your lance, Sir Brian," said Christopher Robin, "maybe I can reach him."

Christopher Robin climbed up as far as he could. Then he held the lance for Piglet to slide safely down.

They all held hands going home. Sir Brian in his heavy suit of armor was their anchor. He walked in the middle so the others wouldn't blow away in the blustery March wind.

"Tonight we look for sky animals," said Owl.

"They're really stars that form animal *shapes*," whispered Rabbit.

"Just look for star shapes in the night sky the way you look for cloud shapes during the day," said Owl.

"I see a lion!" exclaimed Tigger.

"That's Leo," said Owl. "He shines brightest in spring. Did you know there's an animal for each season?"

"I *hope* there's a bear," said Pooh.

9

March Birthday: Pooh

It was Winnie-the-Pooh's birthday and his friends were giving him a party. But Pooh wasn't there!

"How could he forget his birthday?" thought Piglet.

Pooh was at home fixing an afternoon snack. Then he remembered where he should be.

He arrived at the party so out of breath that Tigger and Roo had to blow out the candles.

"Just think," said Pooh, slicing the honey cake Kanga had brought, "I almost *missed* this!"

Poem by Winnie O'Pooh

March Seventeen—
That's the day we all wear green,
To show we wish the Irish
A St. Patrick's Day that's grand-ish!

In spring, paint the house or fence
or perhaps a bird house.

Spring is also a good time
to put away winter clothes.

11

Kite Flying

During the last windy days of March, Pooh and his friends go fly their kites.

The flower for March is the daffodil.

April

April Birthday: Sir Brian

Early in April, everyone was invited to a surprise birthday party for Sir Brian. But no one had any idea who was giving the party.

"Are all those flags and banners flying because it's his birthday?" asked Piglet.

"They look more like rugs and drapes," said Kanga. "I'd say Sir Brian was spring cleaning."

13

When Sir Brian opened the door, he was wearing an apron over his armor and carrying a mop.

"He does look surprised," whispered Pooh.

"Happy birthday!" Out jumped Dragon, shaking with laughter, to lead them in singing "Happy Birthday."

Sir Brian *was* surprised. "I was sure you'd forgotten my birthday, so I started spring cleaning."

"You can do that later," said Dragon. "Come, the party's at my lair!"

In spring, do spring cleaning.

An April Poem

What comes up in April?
Spring flowers.
What comes down in April?
Spring showers!

In spring, plant a garden.

The flower for April
is the sweet pea.

Easter Eggs

Easter comes in the spring—sometimes in March and sometimes in April. At Eastertime Pooh and his friends decorate eggs.

Rabbit

Pooh

Piglet

16

Pooh's Favorite Flower

"April showers bring May flowers," said Pooh, hurrying off to the meadow. "I hope they've brought lots of clover, too."

Sure enough, all the clover was in bloom. This meant there would be lots of honey. Bees make their sweetest honey from the nectar of the tiny, sweet-smelling clover blossoms.

"Thank you," said Pooh to a passing bee.

May

to POOH
from Guess Who?

May 1: May Day

Friends celebrate May Day by giving each other May baskets. It's fun trying to guess who left the basket of flowers at your door.

On the first of May everyone in the Hundred Acre Wood went out very early, carrying a May basket for a special friend. And nobody ran into anybody else until . . .

. . . Pooh ran into Piglet.

"Oh!" exclaimed Pooh. "What a pretty basket!"

"Thank you," said Piglet, wondering how he was going to get it onto Pooh's doorstep. "I like yours, too."

"Thank you," said Pooh, wondering how to get his basket onto Piglet's doorstep.

Finally they just traded baskets right there!

The flower for May is lily of the valley.

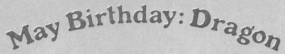

May Birthday: Dragon

The May birthday party was for Dragon. He took up six places at the table. Lots of Rabbit's friends-and-relations came to the party.

Dragon tried and tried to blow out the candles on the cake. But each time he blew, his fiery breath lit up all the candles he had just blown out!

Finally he took a long drink of lemonade to cool his breath. *Then* he blew out the candles—and they *stayed* out!

21

SUMMER

Summer is just full of good things.
In June, July, and August
There's fishing, swimming, and strawberries
And best of all—NO SCHOOL!

June

On the first warm day in June, go on a picnic.*

*What to put in your picnic basket:

Fried chicken, sandwiches, pickles, potato chips, hard-boiled eggs (don't forget salt), watermelon, cherry tomatoes, bananas, apples, oranges, grapes, celery strips, cookies, cake, and a jug of ice-cold lemonade.

Christopher Robin cut very small pieces of cake for the smallest of Rabbit's friends-and-relations at his June birthday party.

Small got lost for ten minutes under a paper hat. He found his way out just in time for a second helping of birthday cake.

Rose is the flower for June.

In summer, listen to the crickets.

24

The Longest Day of the Year always comes in June. Kanga told Roo he could stay up till the end of the Longest Day—*if* he could stay awake.

"I'll take an extra long nap," Roo promised. But by naptime he was too excited to sleep.

Later in the afternoon Roo got sleepy. Tigger tried to help him stay awake.

They ran races.
They played tag.

Tigger even gave Roo bouncing lessons. But it was no use.

At supper Roo fell asleep over his egg custard.

"He'll be so disappointed," said Kanga as she carried him up to bed.

Later, Tigger went to Roo's room. "Wake up," he said. Together they watched the last bit of the Longest Day fade from the window.

"Thank you, Tigger," said Roo. And he went right back to sleep.

In late June the Star Gazers met again.

Owl's porch wasn't big enough to hold Dragon. But by balancing on his tail, he could see quite well from the ground.

"That's me up there!" Dragon exclaimed.

"It's Draco, the Dragon," said Owl. "Rather dim, but a summer sky animal all the same."

In summer, chase fireflies.

July Birthday: Kanga

Rabbit and Tigger made a freezer of lemon ice cream for Kanga's birthday party. Pooh brought a big honey cake. Kanga received a lovely present from Roo—a bouquet of fresh-picked larkspur. Kanga said it was one of her nicest birthdays ever.

Larkspur is the flower for July.

Hundred Acre Wood Records

The most honey ever was eaten by Pooh. Four jars at one sitting followed by five honey combs.

The record high-bounce was made by Tigger—from the ground to the third highest branch of the tallest of the Six Pine Trees.

The highest tree climb was made by Christopher Robin —all the way to the third highest branch of the tallest of the Six Pine Trees, to help Tigger get down.

The record for having the most friends-and-relations is held by Rabbit.

Camping Out

All week long Pooh and Piglet planned their all-night camp-out in Pooh's back yard.

Scooping up their gear, the campers ran inside Pooh's house.

But just as the campers unrolled their sleeping bags and unpacked their sandwiches, raindrops began to fall.

Later, snug in sleeping bags on the floor, Piglet said, "Camping *in* is almost as much fun as camping *out*."

"And a lot drier," said Pooh.

On the Hottest Day of the Year sit in the shade with cold lemonade and think of the Coldest Day.

August

August 15: Hay Fever Season Begins

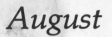

Achoo! 'Tis the season to be sneezin'
What's the reason?
Gesundheit! It's Hay Fever Season!

In summer, water your flowers.   *The flower for August is the gladiola.*

Since Very Small Beetle was so small, the August birthday party was planned especially to suit him.

His punch was served in a thimble so he could drink with no fear of falling in. There were two cakes—a regular birthday cake for everyone else and a cupcake that Small could cut with a doll-size knife.

The tiny blue candle was just right for Small to blow out with one small puff.

More Hundred Acre Wood Records

The record for making the most egg custards in one year: Kanga with 730.

The record for eating the most egg custards in one year: Roo with 730.

The most pecks of pickled haycorns were picked by Piglet. (No one else wanted them.)

The record for talking the longest is held by Owl. Three hours, 45 minutes and 19 seconds on his favorite subject, the very wise Owl family.

The record for being the gloomiest is held by Eeyore—365 days a year. (There are no challengers.)

The record for getting lost is held by Small. Seventeen times in one week.

"Why is fall called fall?" Pooh asked.

"Can't you see?" said Rabbit. "Because it's time for the leaves to fall!"

And a big oak leaf fell right on Pooh's head.

September

September Birthday: Roo

This was a very special birthday for Roo.
"Now I'm old enough to go to school!" he told Rabbit's friends-and-relations at the September party.

He showed them the red lunch box and green satchel Kanga had given him. He could scarcely wait!

The flower for September is the aster.

The First Day of School

In early September, school opens. Tigger was supposed to take Roo to school on Roo's first day. But Tigger forgot.

"I can go by myself," said Roo.

Kanga was about to say she'd better take him when Owl knocked at the door.

"I'm going back to school to brush up on math-e-mat-ics," Owl said. "Could Roo take me?"

Kanga thought that was a fine idea. So did Roo, and off they went to school together.

On his first day Roo learned to count up to six.

And Owl learned that five and six make eleven!

October

The Harvest Season

October was a busy time in the Hundred Acre Wood. It was the Harvest Season, when everybody stored up supplies for winter.

Christopher Robin stored up seeds for the birds from the sunflowers he had planted in the spring. Piglet picked a peck of haycorns.

Rabbit stored carrots, while Eeyore piled up thistles.

Kanga canned vegetables and made jam.

Pooh was the busiest of all. He stored so many pots of honey in his house that the cupboard couldn't hold them all. He piled them in the bookcase, under the table, and in corners.

"My," said Piglet, looking around. "Your house looks like a supermarket, Pooh."

October Birthday: Rabbit

At the October birthday party, Rabbit blew out the candles on the carrot cake, while his friends-and-relations sang Happy Birthday to *their* friend-and-relation, Rabbit.

Small got so excited he fell in the punch bowl. He climbed aboard an ice cube and was rescued at once.

The flower for October is the calendula.

In fall, collect pretty colored leaves.

October 31: Halloween

On Halloween Pooh and Piglet put sheets over their heads and went Trick or Treating.

"Do you think we can really scare Rabbit?" Piglet asked, as they knocked on his door.

"Of course," said Pooh.

The door opened and there grinning at them was a great big orange goblin with flashing eyes!

43

Pooh and Piglet didn't stop running until they got to Pooh's house, where they hid under the bed!

Rabbit took the pumpkin off his head. "They really thought I was a goblin," he said, with a chuckle. He put a candle inside the pumpkin and set it on the windowsill.

For Halloween, make a jack o'lantern.

November

"How can a woolly bear give a weather report?" asked Piglet.

"Easy," said Pooh, "if the woolly bear is a caterpillar. When its black stripes are wider than its orange stripes, that means a very cold winter is coming. . . . Or is it the other way around, I wonder?"

Piglet didn't know and the woolly bear wouldn't say.

"We'll know soon," said Pooh. Winter is almost here."

In fall, watch the birds fly south.

In November the Star Gazers had another meeting. When
Pooh looked through Owl's telescope, he was afraid he was
seeing double.

"I see *two* bears up there!" he said.

"That's right," said Owl. "Big Bear and Little Bear are the
twin sky animals for fall."

In fall, rake leaves.

November Birthday: Piglet

It was getting too chilly for outdoor parties, so the November birthday party for Piglet was held in Kanga's warm and cozy kitchen. Everyone, including some of Rabbit's friends-and-relations, toasted Piglet with hot chocolate and whipped cream.

The flower for November is the chrysanthemum.

Winter's cold brings us ice and snow.
We jump on our sleds and go, go, go!

48

December

After the first winter snowfall, go outside and build a snowman.*

*What to put on your snowman:

stones for eyes
carrot for a nose
pebbles for a mouth
twigs or small branches for arms
stones for buttons
hat and scarf
a broom

HUNNY

December Birthday: Owl

Rabbit and Kanga planned a special party for Owl's birthday in December—a Trim the Tree Party.

Everyone gathered around a tall, snow-covered tree in Kanga's yard.

"We're trimming this tree with food for our bird friends who don't fly south," said Owl. "It's to thank them for the cheerful songs they bring us all winter long."

Kanga and Roo hung baskets of seeds on the tree limbs. Owl flew up to loop strings of popcorn in the branches.

When Owl and the others went back inside, the grateful bird friends held their own party in the branches of the tree trimmed just for them.

The shortest day in the year comes in December. Pooh felt as if he had barely gotten up before it was time to go to bed again.

The December flower is the narcissus.

December 24: Christmas Eve

On Christmas Eve everyone in the Hundred Acre Wood went out to sing Christmas carols. The night was dark, but Dragon lit the way with his fiery breath.

Their last stop was the castle, where Sir Brian welcomed them with mugs of hot chocolate. From inside the castle came the crackle of burning yule logs.

As the carolers started home, Sir Brian called out, "And to all a good night!"

January

January 1: New Year's Day

Pooh tried on the red sweater he'd gotten for Christmas. He couldn't button it.

"Piglet," he said, "I'll have to make a New Year's re-so-lu-tion."

"What's that?" asked Piglet.

Pooh held up one paw. "I, Winnie the Pooh, resolve to eat less honey this year so I will lose weight around my tummy."

"I hear that honey poured over snow tastes as good as an ice-cream sundae," said Piglet.

Pooh thought·for a minute. "Snow isn't fattening," he said, taking down a pot of honey. "Let's try it."

In winter, wear warm clothes.

On the Coldest Day of the Year,
throw another log on the fire and
think of the Hottest Day.

January Birthday: Tigger

At the January birthday party, Tigger introduced Rabbit's friends-and-relations to a delicious new dessert—Extract of Malt Sundaes. (It was really Roo's Strengthening Medicine poured over snow.) Small found it a bit sticky. Tigger had no trouble eating six helpings.

The flower for January is the carnation.

In January Rabbit brought along several of his relations to the Star Gazers' meeting. That wasn't surprising since their own relation, Lepus the hare, was up there in the winter sky.

February

February 14: St. Valentine's Day

On Valentine's Day Piglet left
a very special Valentine for Pooh.

Dear Winnie-the-Pooh,
Sweaters are red,
Mufflers are blue,
Honey is sweet,
And this Valentine's
for you!

The flower for February is the violet.

February Birthday: Eeyore

It had to happen to Eeyore—being born on February 29th. Everyone knows that February 29th comes only once every four years.

"But there's always a February 28th," said Christopher Robin. So that was the date they picked to celebrate Eeyore's birthday, and his friends gave him a very special party. There were even thistles on the cake.

Summer, winter, spring, fall —
What's your favorite one of all?

I like the one that's here this minute.
So come enjoy the fun that's in it!